Revel Street

The Skatepark Kidnapping

Nealie Rose

Mysteries by Nealie Rose:

The Portal in the Attic

The Skatepark Kidnapping

The story begins the day after the end of
The Portal in the Attic...

CHAPTER ONE

"Detective Golden called and said to be sure to read today's newspaper, because there's something in it about last night," Mom said.

Samantha Larson shot out of her kitchen chair. "I'll check!" She hurried to the office off the kitchen. Detective Golden was handling the case about Gerald McIntyre, the man who was arrested for breaking into their house yesterday. She had a cut and a bruise where McIntyre hit her across the face.

Samantha and her 17 year-old sister, Laura, were shoulder-to-shoulder as they stared at the biggest headline of the online Kokomo News:

Young Heir to BCB Plastics Missing

Samantha exclaimed, "What? I thought this was about what happened to us?"

Laura's brows wrinkled as she read,

Mason Smythe, age 11, of Muncie, Indiana disappeared around 10:00 a.m. yesterday morning. The son of Edward and Roberta Smythe, owners of BCB Plastics Corporation, was last seen when his mother dropped him off at Breeze Skatepark in Upland. It was reported he was seen getting into a black Honda CRV in the parking lot. Anyone with any information on the whereabouts of Mason, please call the Muncie Police department at 765-747-5848, or the FBI at 202-324-3000.

Samantha said, "That's awful. That's the skatepark I want to go to. Do you think someone helped him run away?"

Laura answered, "Probably, but if the FBI's involved, maybe they think he was kidnapped. Look, here's our story at the bottom of the page . . ."

Local Family Attacked by Ex Con

Zeke and Jay Munro of 2212 Revel St. came to the aid of Samantha and Laura Larson of 2214 Revel St.

Nobody was seriously harmed. Parolee Gerald McIntyre has been charged with two counts of kidnapping, assault, felony hand gun violation, and breaking and entering at 2214 Revel Street, Kokomo. McIntyre previously served time in Indiana State Prison for bank robbery and murder. He has been out of prison less than a year. Detective Al Golden of the Kokomo Police stated that more charges may follow, but could not elaborate at this stage of the investigation.

Samantha said, "That's it? This doesn't say anything about the $10,000 reward. Zeke and Jay have to get it if it's still there."

Laura added, "I hate to think what would have happened to us."

———————————

Next door, Jay and Zeke Munro, 13 and 15, couldn't talk about anything but what happened the previous night.

Jay sat in Zeke's room on the floor with his back to a wall. "I could tell Mom and Dad didn't want to go to work today. Dad was yawning like crazy."

Zeke had his back against the headboard on his bed and his legs stretched out. "Can't blame them. We were lucky to get to sleep in. Christmas break's almost over, and what a break we've had! I feel like it's been months, not a couple weeks."

Jay wondered, "Do you think we'll be popular when we get back to school? It was in the news this morning."

Zeke said, "Really? What did it say?"

"Online news just had the basics, but it said we helped save Laura and Sam. And it made McIntyre sound like a real mean killer. Yeah, we'll probably be school heroes."

Zeke shook his head. "I bet nobody there even reads the news. We could've been

4

shot, you know. Sam and Laura could be dead, too. Dad couldn't say it last night because of Mom, but that dude shot four people point blank here at our house. He was seriously demented."

Jay added, "And that bank teller. That's five people. I don't know how you did it –you know, going up there so fast to stop him. Weren't you scared? Heck, I just followed you because I knew something was up. If I'd known *what...*"

"Are you saying you wouldn't have followed me if you knew?" Zeke hadn't stopped to think about Jay when he rushed to the attic.

Jay didn't look at Zeke when he said, "Maybe not. I don't know. I've always been kind of chicken. Not a dare-devil like you."

"Listen, Jay, I'm older than you. I'm bigger than you. I'm the oldest. Those things may make me seem like some tough guy, but I get scared sometimes, too."

"You don't act like it."

Zeke laughed, "You want to know something funny that scared me?"

"Yeah, sure." Jay was all ears.

"Sam Larson scared me really bad when I first saw her in our attic. I acted angry. I thought I was angry, but maybe she scared me. Imagine being scared by little Sam."

Jay stared at Zeke a little too long, and Zeke barked, "What?"

Jay responded, "She's really cute."

Zeke picked up a pillow and threw it hard at Jay on the floor. "I tell you something serious to make you feel better, and you gotta talk about girls." He swung his legs off the bed and stomped to his closet for clothes. His phone rang.

It was Laura Larson. He said, "Hi. How are you and Sam?"

Laura said, "Sam's face is kinda purple on one side, no concussion, and I'm sore, but we're good! Thank you SO MUCH! Can you *believe* the bank money was found in our attic wall?"

Zeke asked, "Can we get together and talk? I mean, you and Sam were attacked by a murderer, and I broke his arm, but could we talk in person?"

Laura replied, "Sure. My parents came back from their trip late last night, so can we meet at your house?"

Zeke answered, "Not a good idea. Mom and Dad both had to work today. They have rules."

Laura said, "Okay. Since you're not from around here, you might not know there's a small Community Center that we could walk to. It has tables and vending machines. How about there?"

He said, "Great. Meet you outside in ten minutes." Zeke turned to Jay and said, "Hurry and get dressed. And you don't need to put on a bunch of smell-good."

Jay jumped up and hurried off. "Just one shot of it. You'd be smart to use some, too."

Zeke had to laugh after Jay ran out to get ready. Jay sure could irritate him, but he was glad he had him. *I'm not telling him that, though.*

CHAPTER TWO

The four of them met out on the sidewalk. Despite the all the snow the day before, the roads and sidewalks were mostly clear. Zeke couldn't help but notice the bandage on Sam's cheek. "Wow, that looks painful," he said as he and Jay walked with them.

Sam gave a tiny smile and said, "I can't laugh or yawn without hurting. We might have got killed if you and Jay hadn't come through in time. That guy was old, but he was really strong."

Jay blurted, "Anything for you two!"

Zeke glared at Jay and said, "It was intense. What exactly happened?"

Laura jumped in. "Sam and I were watching movies in the dark. McIntyre appeared out of nowhere and grabbed me! Then Sam jumped on him!" Laura put her arm around Sam's shoulder. "He hit her across the face and knocked her down."

Jay looked at Sam and said, "Seriously? You went after him? You are pretty, but you're awful skinny. You're *brave!*"

Zeke whistled low, "You sure are, Sam. Brave, that is –I don't mean skinny."

Sam started to laugh and stopped walking to grab her face. "Ouch...ouch...I can't laugh. It hurts too much."

Laura continued, "He dragged us to the bathroom and blocked it with a chair. I texted you first, because I knew you could use the portal. Then I called 911. I heard McIntyre going upstairs and walking around above us for a minute. I didn't hear anything else, except for sirens. I wasn't sure if he went from the second floor to the attic, but I thought he was headed to the attic to get that gun we found. Then I got REALLY scared."

Zeke followed them to the Community Center. He liked these neighbors. Maybe Indiana wouldn't be so bad after all. A large one-story building with bushes all around it was up ahead.

Laura commented, "It's not much, but it has furniture, vending, foosball, pool, and one arcade game. Behind the building there's a small cement skatepark, basketball court, and playground equipment."

Zeke said, "Did you say skatepark?"

Jay added, "I thought there weren't any around here?"

Sam said, "Nothing indoor, and it's winter. It's also low budget. And small."

Zeke responded, "Hmm. I want to see it before we go in."

Behind the building Zeke saw a small area with some inclines and half bowls with snow on them. "This is way better than nothing. We'll use it when the snow's gone. We can go in now."

Laura led the way to metal chairs around a table. She said, "All they have in the machines is pop, chips, and candy bars."

Jay asked, "Any black licorice or Zero bars?"

Zeke rolled his eyes. Jay always had food on his mind. The girls sat down and he watched Jay get a root beer and a bag of M&M's.

To his credit, when Jay sat down he held out the bag of candy and announced, "I got this so we could share."

"Thanks." Laura held her hand out.

Sam said, "No thanks, Jay. Tell us how things happened last night."

Jay took a gulp of pop. "I saw Zeke tearing up to the attic with his baseball bat, and he wasn't stopping for anything. I had no idea what was was going on, so I grabbed my bat and followed him. Zeke hit McIntyre with the bat because he had a gun."

Zeke added, "I hadn't planned on breaking his arm, but he went for the gun."

Jay said, "Then the cops were there and took over."

Sam asked, "So you got Laura's text to come help us?"

Zeke answered, "Uh, actually, no. My phone was in my garage, and I was heading out to get it when I saw big footprints in the snow. They were going toward *your* house. I knew in my gut it was Gerald McIntyre. I ran in, got my bat, Jay followed, and the rest is history."

Sam had watery eyes. She said, "I prayed to God that we would be rescued. And He sent you two. Thank you."

Zeke nodded.

Jay gushed, "Anything for the Larson's. Call for us any time of day or night."

Sam started to giggle. "Ouch..."

Laura smiled, "Jay, you are too much. I hope there's still a reward. You both deserve to get it for your heroism."

Zeke commented, "Detective Golden said he'd check on it, but if we do get a reward we're sharing it with you."

Laura said, "I'm not getting my hopes up. Hey, did you hear about the eleven-year-old boy who's missing? Somebody saw him getting into a car at Breeze Skatepark yesterday morning."

Zeke said, "No, never heard about that. Eleven is kinda young. Do you know him?"

Sam responded, "No."

Zeke said, "Speaking of Breeze Skatepark, I was going to ask my Mom if she'd take us to there tomorrow. Would you want to go with us?"

Sam whispered, "Yes!!"

Laura laughed, "That would be fun."

CHAPTER THREE

On the way back, Zeke walked beside Laura on Revel Street's shoveled sidewalks. Jay and Sam were several feet ahead. They were almost to their houses when Zeke heard running feet and saw a blur in his side vision, and *WHAM!* – He was knocked into the snow!

Laura stumbled and screamed.

David Mellon yelled, "I'm gonna get you, Zeke! Awful, mean Zeke!"

Zeke was furious. *It's happening again!* He realized then that he had no choice but to apologize for something another "Zeke" did fifty-some years ago, or he would be attacked forever by David Mellon. Zeke sprang up from the snow and put his hands out. "Stay right there, David. I have something to say to you. I'm sorry, David. I'm sorry. *Really sorry*. I didn't mean to be nasty to you when you were little. What can I do to make things better?"

Sam said slowly, "Hi David. Let's be nice. We'll be your friends. Don't hurt Zeke anymore. See, he said he's sorry."

Zeke knew nothing about this special-needs man who lived a few houses away on Revel Street, except that many years ago there was a boy named Ezekiel who was mean to David when he was young. And that particular "Zeke" actually lived in the same house where he and Jay now lived, which made things even worse.

David's eyes were mistrustful. He said, "You're sorry? You took my candy. You took my ball. Give my ball back. Give me my candy back."

Zeke thought fast. "Alright, I'll get some and bring it to you, okay?" He looked around. "Where is Mrs. French, your helper? Let's walk you back home, David."

David hesitated and wouldn't take Zeke's out-stretched hand.

Jay played along and led towards David's house. "Yes, we can take you home." He waved to Sam and Laura, who had inched toward their own house.

Zeke said to them, "I'll let you know about tomorrow. Bye." He smiled at David and coaxed him back to his home using hand motions while he talked soothingly. "David, I will be your friend. I am going to take you home, and then I'll go get some candy for you."

David followed Zeke and Jay back to his yellow house, but he did not smile. He seemed uncertain about trusting Zeke.

Once David was deposited back into the care of an apologetic Mrs. French, who said she had been so absorbed in a TV show that she didn't know David had left.

As soon as they got back home, Zeke wiped off his boots and ran into the kitchen. "Hey, Mom, I'll explain later. Or Jay can tell you. Gotta grab some candy. Back soon!"

Zeke felt stupid knocking at the yellow house while he held a bag of candy.

Mrs. French answered. "Oh, I'm sorry about what happened earlier." She looked over her shoulder and said, "Are you sure you should be here?"

"Yes, I think I need to make peace with David, for what the other kid –uh, Ezekiel– did to him a long time ago. I brought chocolate for him. He's allowed to have it, isn't he?"

"Yes. Come in and I'll call him."

David followed behind her when she returned. She had evidently briefed him about his visitor, because David said, "You have chocolate for me?"

Zeke said, "Yes." He held out the bag.

"Snickers! I like Snickers!" David's smile was ear to ear. he took the bag and ripped it open to get to one of the miniature bars.

"I want to be nice to you. I'm sorry. I will get a ball for you, too, as soon as I can. What color do you like?"

David said, "Orange. Basketballs are orange. You took my basketball."

Zeke wondered *what else did I do before I was born?* But he just said, "Oh wow, I never should have done that. I have one at home. Let me run and get it. Here, take this candy. Be right back."

Zeke zipped home and ran to the garage to find a basketball. He hoped Jay's was out there. He found it and went back to David's house and knocked again.

This time David answered. Mrs. French was behind him. "Basketball!" he almost shouted. After taking it from Zeke, David turned it in his hands. "This is not my ball. My ball says DAVID."

Zeke's heart sank. "Oh no, wrong ball. I will find it. It may take a couple days, but I'll find it." He said goodbye and walked home with Jay's ball.

Jay was in the living room when he walked in, and said, "Hey, what are you doing with my basketball?"

"Sorry. I took it to that David guy to try to make peace with him, but he said his ball has his name on it, and he didn't want this one. Great."

"What? I don't believe it, Zeke! You were going to *give my basketball away without asking me?*"

Zeke rubbed his forehead and temple. "Yeah. I guess I was. Sorry."

Jay glared at him. "Thanks a lot."

Zeke needed a nap. He headed for the stairs and mumbled again that he was sorry. *Sorry that David thinks I'm that other Ezekiel. Sorry that he attacked me again. Sorry that I took Jay's basket ball. Sorry it didn't have DAVID written on it. Sorry that I have to say sorry! What was I thinking?*

———————————

That evening after Zeke and Jay's dad got home from his store The Fill Me Up, Jay put his hands together like he was praying and said, "There's a new indoor skatepark about forty-five minutes from here in Upland. Zeke called them and they sound like they're strict with the rules, so you guys should like it. Can we please go tomorrow? Break ends soon, and we are *dying* to ride our boards. Please…"

Dad looked at Mom and said, "I have to work. What do you think?"

She asked, "What is the set-up there?"

"They have a resident pro, a skate shop, half pipes, ramps, a bowl, equipment rentals, and helmets are required." Zeke got wound up just telling her about it.

Dad asked, "BMX?"

"Yes, and they have a whole separate area for little kids who are learning, and I never heard of that before. So how bad can it be? It's called Breeze Skatepark. 1330 Market Street in Upland. I have the phone number."

Dad said, "Wait a minute. That's the place where a boy disappeared yesterday morning."

"He was dropped off in the parking lot, got in a car and left. I don't see how you can hold that against the skatepark, Dad," Zeke said.

Dad nodded and said, "How about I see what I can find out about that section of town. I'll let you know after I do my own checking tonight."

Jay responded, "I'm sure you'll be okay with it, Dad. We want to take Sam and Laura with us, so they want to go, too."

"Sam and Laura?" Dad scratched the back of his neck. "Circumstances have thrown you all together. When I think what could have happened to them last night." He sighed and sat down. "Okay, I'll check and as long as there is no history of police visits to the place for partying or violence, it will be okay to go."

"WHOOP!" Jay jumped and high-fived Zeke, who was smiling, too.

CHAPTER FOUR

The next day was Friday, December 28th and Samantha and Laura were invited to go with Zeke and Jay to Breeze Skatepark at 9:15 a.m. The boys' mother, Darci Munro, would drive them.

While Laura was getting ready to go, her sort-of boyfriend, Kyle, called her again about another movie date, but she put him off until after the first part of the New Year. That was when she hoped life would return to normal, because the portal should be closed then. But how could she tell him *that*? She couldn't. He would think she was crazy. Nobody would believe it. That's what stunk about the portal.

Ever since Zeke told her yesterday that they would share reward money with her and Sam, Laura couldn't help but daydream about it.

Will the reward really come through? I wonder how much money it will be if it does? I wonder if their parents will let them share it with us?

Laura had been buying collectible items for the last couple years and storing them at her grandmother's. She used babysitting money and shopped at thrift stores and garage sales. Her mother had contributed some cool things to her growing collection, too. *Reward money would make my dream so much more attainable...please, God, please..."*

She decided to leave her hair down and wear a teal shirt with jeans and tall brown fringed boots to the skatepark.

When Sam called out, "Are you ready?" Laura bounded down the steps and saw her sister had on a T-shirt, jeans and running shoes. Sam said, "Too bad I told Dad we are just watching Jay and Zeke. I'd like to try it. Maybe next time."

Zeke was already in the front seat and Jay held the door open for the girls. Laura climbed in first and Sam sat in the middle.

Zeke's mom said, "Hi girls. Oh, Samantha, that looks like it hurts. How are you doing?"

Zeke turned around in his seat and said, "Hey."

Sam said, "Hi. It hurts if I touch my face or move my mouth too much."

Jay said, "Mmm, somebody smells good."

Glancing over at Mom, Zeke rolled his eyes and she grinned back.

Sam responded, "You are so funny, Jay. Its coconut-lime lotion."

Jay said, "I like it. You guys planning to watch, or do you want to try it today?"

Laura said, "My parents aren't too excited about us skateboarding. I honestly wouldn't do it anyway, but I love watching. Sam wants to have some lessons, but hasn't cleared it yet with our parents."

Sam asked, "How long have you guys been at it?"

Mom spoke up as she drove, "Zeke's been riding since about eight, and that's when Jay started copying him. They just messed around outside, and we'd go to small outdoor skateparks so they could practice."

Zeke added, "We do ramps, bowls, platforms or ledges, half pipes, and rails. But we don't do real street-skating because it's too dangerous. Our parents want to keep us alive."

Sam asked, "So, what's a half-pipe?"

Jay answered by holding his thumbs and index fingers in a circle. "Okay, pretend this is a huge pipe. Cut it in half *long-way* and it's a half-pipe you can skate in. Only bigger, of course."

Laura asked, "What's the most dangerous thing about street-skating?"

Zeke poked his head around to the back and said dryly, "Cars. Also people, cats, dogs. Nothing is fixed. You just never know. They say that if you get hit by a car you're supposed to go up, not down. Haven't figured out yet exactly how that's supposed to happen. A lot of parks have a set-up with stairs and ledges and stuff that simulate a street, but to really skate the street you gotta be half crazy."

Mom turned to Zeke and smiled as she said, "Why don't you tell them what Detective Golden called about this morning?"

Laura asked, "He called you today?"

Jay piped up, "Yeah! Wait till you hear."

Zeke said, "We were going to tell you when you got in the car, but we got to talking about other stuff. There really is reward money when McIntyre is convicted." He looked at the girls and motioned with his eyes toward Mom.

He chose his words carefully, because she didn't know *where* the old crimes had been committed. "Detective Golden said he contacted Catherine Bathis, the mother of the murdered kids. She lives in Kentucky. He said she's in her nineties and still sharp, and that she cried when he told her about the arrest of Gerald McIntyre. Her parents put $10,000 in a savings account for a reward back in 1960, and it was not to be touched until somebody was convicted of killing her children. Dad said the actual amount of that would depend on whether it was figured as simple interest or compound interest, and taxes and stuff. Golden said he'd be in touch with her and let us know. McIntyre has to be found guilty, or plead guilty, though. Golden said it looks like McIntyre has basically confessed to everything."

Sam exclaimed, "Awesome! However it's figured, it will be way over $10,000 after all these years. Will you use the reward toward college?"

Laura laughed and added, "That ought to make your move to Indiana worth it."

Zeke responded, "We talked to Mom and Dad and they agree. Like I said yesterday, if the reward eventually comes through, we're splitting it four ways, and you and Sam get a share."

Sam objected, "We didn't have anything to do with catching him –you guys did it."

Mom said firmly, "If there is a reward, my sons are splitting it with you. Think about it. You were in this with them when that creep came into your house, because if that hadn't happened they couldn't have saved you."

Sam said, "Well that would be nice, but I wouldn't want to count my chickens before they're hatched."

Jay burst out laughing, "You sure say some weird things in Indiana! Awesome 'possum, and hatching chickens? I know you don't have a farm. Do you even have a *garden*?"

She said, "Of course not."

Cackling like a lunatic, Jay soon had them all laughing. The forty-five minute drive went quickly with everyone talking.

CHAPTER FIVE

They found the place easily enough. The numbers 1330 were plastered across the front of the huge building, so there was no missing it. The sign had a picture of a skateboard on it, and BREEZE was painted on the deck of the skateboard. The building was huge and looked like it had been a factory or a warehouse at one time. There was an Arby's down the street. Not much else.

When they arrived a little after ten, the place was opening for the day. There were other cars already in the parking lot and people were getting their equipment and bikes out.

Zeke saw that some of the kids going in were really young. The places they'd been used to were for older kids and young adults, and he hoped the little kids had their own area like they said on the phone when he called.

Zeke and Jay got out of the Enclave and pulled their boards and helmets out of the back. They already had on their Duffs skate shoes. It was slippery as they headed to the entrance.

For Zeke, this was a fantastic day after five weeks of wishing he was back in Phoenix. Sure, he still wished he was back there and hadn't moved to Indiana, but today there was a skateboard to ride, new friends that he liked and could count on, and even reward money on the horizon. He was happy.

They entered the lobby and then went into a large area that served as a skate shop store. While disco music played, people lined up to pay, and sign waivers at the counter if it was their first time. Zeke glanced around at the clothes, backpacks, helmets, board, and bike parts for sale, as the check-in line moved forward.

Zeke looked at Jay. "Interesting place, huh?"

Jay asked, "'Sup with the music?" He started to do some disco moves right there in line next to Mom.

Zeke casually said, "You've found your niche, Bro."

As the line moved forward, Zeke thought the guy taking money behind the cash register looked like he could be an actor cast as Jesus in a skatepark stage play. He had a knit hat pulled down over long brown hair and a curled-up handlebar mustache. *I doubt Jesus had a handlebar...*Zeke noted the little kids were bypassing his line totally, and going off down a hall with their parents, and he sighed with relief.

Sam joked, "Hey, if I could go with them I might be able to learn how to ride a skateboard."

Mom commented, "The sport is not for everybody. This place is different because of the little kids here. They must give lessons, and Christmas break is a good time to take some."

There was a sign that said admission was $10.00 if you were skating or riding a BMX. $3.00 to watch. Mom commented, "I bet charging people just to watch keeps a lot of trouble out of here."

Zeke and Jay held their scuffed-up helmets and when it was their turn at the register, the guy who looked like Jesus noticed Sam's banged-up face and asked her, "Did that happen skating?"

Sam answered, "No. An old man smacked me and knocked me down."

The guy's expression never changed, but one side of his handlebar mustache twitched. He said, "That's heavy."

Jay hung his arm over Sam's shoulder and said, "I saved her."

Sam added, "It was in yesterday's news, but the Mason Smythe disappearance took front and center on the news. Did you know him?"

Zeke thought Sam sounded like a private detective. She sure wasn't afraid to talk to people.

"Yes, he was here a lot since we opened. He never caused any trouble, but he did brag a lot about his parents and money. I wouldn't be surprised if somebody kidnapped him for ransom. But nobody's asking me."

Mom signed waivers and thanked the guy, and they headed down a hall and around a corner. They walked into a huge area that opened to another big room with ramps, steps, rails, half pipes, and vert ramps. Zeke saw a guy going down into a bowl in the big room ahead of them. There were a half dozen people already in there using bikes and skateboards. All the walls were covered with bright spray paint art and ads for products and events.

Mom found a seating area and sat down with Laura and Sam on a bench that had a sturdy fence in front of it, obviously to protect them from psycho boards and bikes. The room vibrated with music and the sound of wheels and bearings.

As soon as he pulled his helmet on over his head, Zeke felt like he was in Phoenix again, happier than he'd been in a long time. He warmed up and skated to a long course that had a ledge alongside a raised platform. He planted his left foot near the back of the board and powered off with his right. Once he was going so fast that he could put both feet on the board, he flew up the incline and jumped with the skateboard up onto the edge of the ledge, which is called doing an "ollie." He rolled along on it until he reached the downhill side, then he jumped it back down to the other side of the ramp. He was all over the place, just riding the park and trying out everything. His favorite was the bowl, and when he got to it he swooped down in with adrenaline pumping. He sped down to the bottom and back up the other side to the top and tried to head back down, but lost his board and slid to the bottom on his butt.

He loved skating, and couldn't believe how much he'd missed it. He grabbed his board and began to ride the bottom of the bowl, gaining momentum until he was all over it again, up one side and down another.

———————————————

Samantha knew she would learn how to skate, even if she had to go in with the little kids. She just had to, because she was totally taken in.

Darci Munro talked with her and Laura for a while, explaining things. Samantha and Laura eventually carefully wandered around watching, and saw Jeremy Ting come in. He was a friend of Laura's, thin with ebony skin and short braids that stuck out all over. He gave Laura a quick hug. "Hey what are you doin' here, girl?"

"I'm here with my sister Samantha, and my neighbors. None of us have been here before."

Samantha said hi to Jeremy. "And here comes one of the guys who live next to us."

Zeke had picked up his board and was walking over to them. "Hi," he said.

Jeremy said, "I've been in the other room, but I was watching you some. I've seen you at school, too. Name's Jeremy Ting."

Zeke smiled and said, "Zeke Munro. I have a little brother here somewhere."He turned to Samantha and asked, "Is that my water bottle you're holding?"

Samantha said, "Yep, your mom told me to hang onto it for you. Laura has Jay's water." She held it out to him.

Zeke thanked her and drank until it was half gone.

Laura said, "Jeremy, Zeke's new in Indiana. Only been here five weeks."

The guys talked for a minute and Jeremy said he wanted to warm up, and he went off on his board.

Laura said to Zeke, "If you're resting a minute, I need to talk to you about something." She glanced over to where his mother was sitting.

Samantha wondered what Laura wanted to talk about.

"I got a minute," Zeke said as he downed more gulps of water and took his helmet off.

Laura asked, "What are you guys doing for New Year's Eve?"

He shook his head and sighed, "Well, my parents will probably go out to eat at some restaurant. Jay and I will stay home and order pizza, and when they get back we'll watch movies, play cards, or use the Xbox. They aren't partiers." Glancing around, he lowered his voice and added, "You know, I had a great idea for the portal before it closes."

There was a gleam in his eyes and his jaw was set. Zeke intrigued Samantha, because he was definitely a thinking person who was reliable and balanced. Of course she'd only known and talked to him for eight or nine days, but they were an extraordinary eight or nine days, and Zeke had stopped Gerald McIntyre. She wondered if having a brother was similar to having Zeke around. He never seemed to try and impress her or show off. He was just a person. Jay, on the other hand... Jay was funny and approachable, but he seemed to want to get too cozy, based on all the silly things he'd say to her and Laura, but he was nice, too.

Zeke pushed his sweaty blond bangs straight back and whispered to them, "I'd like to skate through the portal before it closes."

Laura blinked and smiled. "Wow. I bet you could do it New Year's Eve. That's what I was asking about –if you guys could come over that night. Our parents will be out probably until 1:00 in the morning, and they like you guys because of what you did to help us. I think they'd agree to a couple hours if your parents do, too."

Zeke looked puzzled. "Why aren't you going out with friends or to a party?"

Laura crossed her arms in front and shifted her weight. She whispered, "You know, I can't seem to move forward on *anything* because of the portal. Zeke, I *pray* it closes for good soon."

Samanatha added, "Me too."

There was a pause before Zeke responded, "I guess I haven't minded because I haven't had a life to get on *with*. Try changing states sometime. You are the only people I consider friends." He shrugged, "If we come over with pizza while my parents eat out, and only stay till they get back, I think they'd be fine with it. They should be gone about two hours – not sure when yet. Then Jay and I can use the portal with our boards. You okay with that?" His blue-green eyes looked hopeful.

Laura bit her lower lip a second and then said, "Wouldn't it be crazy if we caught it on video as you came through?" Her eyebrows went up and she smiled.

He asked, "Who would we show it to? How would we explain it if someone else saw it?"

Samantha said, "Hmm, that could be a problem, Laura, but it's a cool idea."

Samantha saw Darci Munro heading their way. Darci said, "Jay's in the half-pipe. I'm going to leave now and do some shopping about fifteen miles from here. I found a K-Mart, and I'll get lunch while I'm exploring Indiana. Arby's is near when you get hungry. So you'll either be here or at Arby's. Nobody leaves by themselves, and no leaving to go anyplace but Arby's, got it? I'm serious about that because of that missing boy. We don't really know what happened to him, and I don't want you guys to take any chances."

Samantha nodded yes.

Laura said, "Absolutely."

Zeke responded, "Yes, got it. I'm headed back over to the bowl in a minute, but we were just talking, and wonder if we could take pizza over to the Larson's on New Year's Eve while you and Dad go out to eat? We'd come back when you got home."

Darci asked, "What about your parents? Where will they be?"

Laura said, "They are going to my Dad's best friend's house for a big party. Every year they do that. I think they'd be okay with it, since it would only be for a couple hours, and it's safer than being out on the road."

Darci smiled. "That sounds okay, but I need to clear it with your mom first. And I'll check with Mike."

"Great," Zeke said as he put his helmet back on, stepped onto his board and rolled away.

Samantha watched him and Jay a while before her mind drifted to reward money. *What would I do with reward money?* She thought about a car fund or college. Maybe skateboard lessons.

Then her mind drifted to the new start-up church she heard about from her friend, Kelly. It was in a small building only two blocks from her house, and she'd be able to walk instead of having to rely on rides to get all the way to Kelly's church.

Samantha knew a few of the people who were going there, and she wanted to go soon and check it out. Maybe she'd donate some money to the church. The thought made her smile.

CHAPTER SIX

Victor, the kidnapper:

I have never been a criminal. But I have a criminal's brain, because I'm always thinking of ways to make money the easy way. And working at Breeze is not it. I may be co-manager with Bob, but the owner, who lives in a fancy house in Muncie pays us only pennies. Definitely not what I'm worth, considering I'm the resident pro skater here.

So, can you blame me when I see this rich kid start coming here to skate? He's known all over for his parent's money, and he likes to brag about it, too. The little twit thinks he's tough stuff. Well, he used to. Now he's scared.

I wonder what he thinks about all day locked in that office? I know he didn't get a look at me. I haven't uttered a sound, so he can't have any idea it was me that snatched him. Does he know he's being held for ransom money?

Nothing about me is impressive, except the way I skate. I thought about it, too. If I was like 6'3" I would stand out, or if I was 220 pounds or something. But no, I'm just a normal height and weight kind of guy. I just blend in with everyone, and that's highly in my favor.

To tell the truth, I'm scared, too. Scared Bob will be on to me, or the FBI. There's no going back, though. A plan hatched in my head when I stumbled onto the ceiling space. A light fixture in the men's room was shorting out. I have to do the maintenance here, so I took the tile down to look at the light from above. When I was looking up there, I noticed a light source filtering from a crawlspace going along the ductwork.

I decided to see where it was coming from, and crawled along until I reached the end of the line. From my high perch there I looked down on a gigantic empty warehouse lit by natural light from high windows. And there was a wall ladder that took me down the wall into it.

I could tell it wasn't being used because there was dust on everything. There was an office with no window. That was when I began thinking about kidnapping Mason Smythe for a ransom. A lot. I wanted a million bucks, and I knew his parents had it.

Over the next week, I put a new lock on the warehouse office door and threw a blanket in there. I may be the pro skater, but I'm also in charge of emptying trash cans, cleaning the bathrooms, and stocking Breeze, so it was easy for me to carry what I needed for my plan into the men's bathroom.

I put things in trash bags. Crackers, bottled water and a camping toilet for the kid. I hid food, a ski mask, gloves, and a knife on top of ceiling tiles that I crawled by to get to the wall ladder. I stored a narrow lightweight ladder from the warehouse up there, too, to make it easier getting up into the ceiling from the men's bathroom.

It didn't look like anyone had been at the warehouse for a long time, but I didn't want to leave anything in plain sight, just in case.

After I had everything set, I decided to explore every inch of the warehouse before I grabbed the kid. It all looked good, except there was one door that bothered me because it was locked, and I didn't know where it went. So I got the doorknob and lock off and took a look.

It was at the bottom of a cement staircase that went up to a janitor's closet in one of the Breeze hallways. The door at the top was locked, too. I put new locks on both of the staircase doors and put the keys on my personal key ring. I already had a set of keys to everything else at Breeze, and so did Bob the co-manager. The owner in Muncie hardly ever comes around. I guess he's got all kinds of businesses to oversee, and he trusts me and

Bob. Stupid man. If I ever own businesses, I'll be checking on them all the time.

I felt that the staircase could definitely complicate things, but now I was the only person with keys to it, it was all good.

I made friends with Mason. Because I'm the resident pro at Breeze, kids look up to me. I mean, I'm hands-down the best rider.

I decided that on December 26th I would make my move. Mason trusted me. I told him if he came an hour early, I'd work with him for a lesson before we opened. I did that with other kids during the week, either before we opened or after we closed. Nothing unusual. Mason's mother dropped him off that day and sped away in her Jag. I stayed out of sight and hurried from the lobby into the building when I saw Mason headed for the entrance. I had on my ski mask, coat, and gloves. When Mason came through the lobby he yelled, "Hey Vic! I'm here."

I grabbed him from behind, slapped a piece of duct tape over his mouth and pulled a stocking cap over his face. I shoved him through the store and down the little kids' hall to the janitorial closet. He must have been really scared, because he didn't even try to fight back. I had my knife ready if I needed to scare him into complying. I'd made up my mind that he would never hear my voice or see my face. With my face and hands covered, there was no way he could positively identify me if things went bad. But I was pretty sure my scheme would work and I'd end up rich.

I forced Mason down the cement staircase and locked him in the warehouse office. The office walls were reasonably sound-proof, and I knew that nobody would be able to hear yelling after I locked him in and he took the duct tape off his mouth.

When I check on him, I have a pillow stuffed in the coat I wear. Makes me look heavy, you know? That will throw him off, too.

The whole thing was easier than I thought it would be, and only took about ten minutes to throw him in the room and lock the door. Then I hurried to call his mother.

I had her number from the waiver she signed when Mason first came to Breeze.

I said, "Mrs. Smythe, This is Victor from Breeze. Mason had a lesson scheduled with me before we opened today. I was in the lobby by the entrance unlocking the place when I saw him get into a Black Honda at the edge of the parking lot near the road. It left. I waited a few minutes before calling you, thinking maybe he and a friend made a breakfast drive-thru run, but they never came back. I'm sorry, but we will still have to charge you for the lesson, even if there was a change of plans for today." (I thought that made it sound like business as usual.)

She said, "What are you saying?"

I repeated, "I saw Mason get into a black Honda at the far edge of our lot and it left. He didn't come for his lesson. . ."

She screamed, "NO! NO! –That can't be! I'm calling the police."

The phone went dead. I knew that the police would question me, but I wasn't overly worried. I don't have a record; I'm respected because I'm the pro; there aren't any cameras in the vicinity to contradict what I said; and it wasn't unusual for a kid to come for a private lesson.

What did scare me was a lie detector test, but if nobody suspected me, that wouldn't happen. After all, I called Mrs. Smythe right away to report the no-show. When the call was finished, I double-bagged Mason's red helmet and skateboard, then quickly stored them up in the ceiling crawlspace.

Business as usual.

CHAPTER SEVEN

By noon the place was in full swing, buzzing with the whir and hum of wheels and rattling bolts. Music changed from Bee Gees disco to Jamaican, and then to Beach Boys surf music. People all over were practicing technical tricks, and many fell when their bike or board would flip, which is called credit-carding, but most of them tried again. BMX riders did handlebar 360's midair and flips off the vert ramps. The colorful walls were covered with black tire marks.

The longer Samantha watched, the more she enjoyed being there. More than one guy came over to take a break near Laura and talk to her. Samantha saw that Jeremy Ting and Zeke were talking and getting along great.

She was trying to figure out how she'd convince her parents to let her take lessons. *Maybe Jay can teach me at the place behind the community building once the weather gets better. And if we get reward money, I could offer to pay for everything.* She felt a beating pulse in the place and loved every minute. Temporarily gone were thoughts about her sore face, the portal, and Gerald McIntyre. She decided to look at the prices of equipment and wandered back to the store part of Breeze. There were new and used things, and she started looking in the pre-owned section.

Samantha picked up the nicest-looking used helmet that looked like it would fit and checked inside for a price. No price, but there was a name written in small letters with permanent marker: Mason. Startled, she thought that it might be Mason Smythe's helmet! *The paper said he was eleven. There couldn't be that many Masons that skate here and wear a medium sized helmet.* Sam decided to talk about it with the others at lunch when they went to Arby's, because it was entirely possible he sold it to Breeze long before he disappeared.

Zeke and Jeremy talked back and forth at every opportunity, cheering when one was successful at a stunt, and laughing when they weren't. *Finally, someone who seems normal.* Zeke noticed Laura always had someone talking to her, but he didn't know where Samantha was, and decided if she didn't appear soon, he'd take a minute and make sure she was okay.

After one break, Jeremy bent to pull something off the bottom of his shoe before he stepped on his board. He laughed as he held up a sticky strip of label for a camping toilet, and said to Zeke, "Look what I picked up, and I don't go camping." He peeled it off and threw it in the trash can.

Zeke asked, "Where'd you find that?"

Jeremy said, "Must have been in the bathroom."

Zeke took his helmet off, wiped sweat away and asked, "This place have a drinking fountain? My water's gone."

Jeremy said, "Of course not. You have to buy it. Go to Bob the register guy and he gets it for you. It's a buck a bottle. Ask him for a card, too. You come six times, and the seventh time it's free to get in."

Zeke said, "Thanks." He headed for the front of the place where the store and cash register were. He found Sam looking at skateboards.

She made a funny picture. There was this curly-haired skinny girl, with a banged up face, going through skateboard equipment like she had wiped out on her last board and wanted to find something safer.

"Hey, I wondered where you were. How's your face? We'll be here a few more hours, and if you aren't feeling okay at any time, I can call my mom."

Sam replied, "I took some pain meds this morning, and when we eat lunch it will be time for some more, but thanks, I'm fine."

He said, "I need to get some water at the register; I'll be back in a sec."

"Okay, but when you get back I want to show you something, so don't forget me."

Zeke had to wait until two people were checked in, and then he asked Jesus for two bottles of water.

"That'll be two dollars."

Zeke asked, "Do you own this place? It's nice. Different. I'm Zeke Munro."

The young man said, "Thanks. The owner is never here. I'm Bob. I co-manage Breeze with Victor. I handle all things money and the store, and Vic is the pro skater and does maintenance." He handed over the water. "Here you go. I ride BMX when I'm not on the clock. Hope you keep coming back."

"It's great. Thanks." Zeke pictured Jesus on a BMX. Then he asked Bob for a punch card. "Do people ever say you remind them of anyone?" Zeke put the card in his pocket.

Bob said, "All the time."

"Who?"

"Justin Beiber. With a moustache."

Zeke's jaw slackened. "No kidding?"

Smiling, Zeke turned and headed back toward Sam and found her trying on a shoe.

Zeke said, "You'll never believe the conversation I just had."

She looked up at him as she sat on the floor with the shoe. "What was it about?"

"Who do you think that guy at the counter looks like?"

Sam blinked and thought a second before she said, "Uh, Jesus?"

Zeke started laughing and almost doubled over in hysterics.

"Did I say something wrong?"

"No, sorry. I'll explain later. It's okay..." He straightened up and looked at Sam staring quizzically at him. She was still sitting on the floor holding a shoe. He smiled down at her. "You're serious about this, aren't you?"

She said, "You bet. I'll have to buy used stuff, though. Hey, I want to show you something. Come over here." She got up and led the way to a crate of helmets.

Zeke watched as she dug through about ten helmets, appearing baffled. He asked, "What's wrong?"

She replied, "I don't know what happened to it . . . there was a blue one that was my size, and when I looked inside for the price, I saw a name instead." She lowered her voice. "It had the name Mason written inside in marker, real small."

Zeke stared at her. "Okay. . ."

She whispered, "Mason, as maybe in *Mason Smythe*? And now it's gone. It was only fifteen minutes ago, at the most."

Zeke said, "Hmm. Maybe someone bought it? Let me go ask Bob, the manager. Oh, and here's a water."

Sam grabbed the bottle and thanked him. Zeke walked across the large room and went up to the counter. "Bob, have you sold any helmets in the last half hour?"

Bob said, "I haven't sold anything except water and admissions. Why?"

Zeke said, "My friend over there found one she wanted, but it's gone now."

Bob said, "I can't tell you how many times someone has decided to try out equipment without asking. It's probably on someone's head right now while they skate."

Zeke went over to Sam and repeated what Bob said, and she said, "I'll walk around and look. Go ahead and get back to your skate board."

Samantha went down the hall and around a corner into the main room looking for people wearing blue helmets. She scanned the room filled with about twenty BMX bikes and skaters. Then she went to the next area to check, and returned to find Zeke.

She said, "Nobody's wearing it, Zeke. Somebody must have recognized the helmet when I had it, and then took it when I wasn't looking."

Zeke scratched his chin. "It may not be Mason Smythe's helmet at all. Or he could have sold it to Breeze. But why has it vanished? Since you aren't skating, why don't you wander around and keep your eyes open for it. Check out the kid's area, too, because maybe it would fit one of them. You never know. I'll check back with you in an hour when we go to Arby's."

She was satisfied with that and said, "Sounds good."

Vic froze when he heard someone come into the men's bathroom below him. He was up there hiding the blue helmet. He didn't know who was down there, but realized he'd better stop moving until they were gone.

Vic had seen a girl with curly brown hair looking at Mason's old helmet. At one point Mason had sold it to Breeze, but having someone see anything connecting Mason Smythe to Breeze made Vic nervous, and he decided to hide it in his ceiling crawl space.

He wanted all police questioning to be centered away from Breeze. When he went through the store with his black "trash" bag, he'd popped the helmet inside, and took the locked staircase to the warehouse. Then he climbed up the wall ladder to hide it. He was confident that no police would ever look up there for anything.

The thing that bothered him most was that he hadn't really thought out exactly how to do a ransom note and collect the million dollars without giving himself away. He told himself that Mason wasn't going anywhere, and he would get it figured out.

Vic thought that the longer he waited before sending a ransom note, the more likely it would be that he'd get the cooperation he wanted.

He felt certain that the police would never think to look there. Who gets kidnapped and stays in the same location? He doubted he'd have to move Mason to another place.

At least he hoped he was right.

CHAPTER EIGHT

Mason Smythe:

Mason got to Breeze early that morning, expecting a lesson form Vic the pro skater. He was excited about the private lesson. When a heavyset masked man grabbed him before he could locate Vic at the skatepark, Mason was scared, but not super afraid because he knew Vic had to be nearby and would come to help him. He really looked up to Vic.

But Vic never came. Mason figured Vic had been hit over the head and was lying on the floor somewhere. The guy who'd grabbed him taped his mouth shut, and put a hat down over his face so Mason couldn't see where he was going, but he knew they hadn't gone outside. He was somewhere in the big building, but where? He was shoved down some stairs and made to walk quite a ways before being thrown in this office.

The office was dirty and dusty. There was an old coffee cup with a spoon in it sitting on a desk. A blue blanket was in the corner on the floor, and another corner had a camping toilet and a roll of toilet paper beside it. There had been 22 fresh bottles of water sitting on the dirty desktop with bags of potato chips and some packages of crackers. Mason spent time counting and recounting the water bottles, even as he used them up.

Mason didn't know how long he'd been in the locked office. There was no window to gauge day and night.

He'd already drunk ten bottles of the water. Did that mean when all 22 bottles were empty that he'd be released? Or killed? Was there a reason there were 22 bottles? Would be given more water if he drank all that was there?

Questions and more questions ran through his mind continually as he sat on the floor in the room without a chair. Who was the man who'd put him here? He was sure it wasn't

Vic. Vic was too nice, and he was thin.
Besides, Breeze was in a huge warehouse and
anyone might have access to the places in it. He
hoped Vic was alive.

Mason believed his parent's money was
why he was here. He'd always been proud of
how much money they had, and he bragged a
lot. Now he wished he'd kept his mouth shut.
Maybe he wouldn't be here if he had. How
long would he be here, and would police and
his parents know where to look for him?

Mason had opened the desk drawers,
looking for a letter opener or a pair of scissors
to try to break or remove the doorknob, but the
only things in the desk were a few paper clips,
a rubber band, and an old receipt for a Chinese
food carryout order. It was dated 2014.

That restaurant receipt was all he had to
read, and he looked at it often. Egg rolls, crab
Rangoon, Hunan Beef, Chicken Broccoli, and
wonton soup....Wow, was he hungry for some
of that. The crackers and chips were not filling

him up, and he was afraid to eat too much because there might not be any more.

And the camping toilet...what if that got too full? He didn't want to think on that too long.

Mason was pretty scared the man might come back and hurt him, so he kept thinking about self-defense and what he could do if that happened...

CHAPTER NINE

Darci was at K-Mart when hints of an oncoming migraine appeared. She felt the subtle signs and knew she had to get home as soon as possible. She could not be incapacitated before she got the kids back home. *They are going to be disappointed about having to leave so soon!*

Walking into the noise and motion at Breeze was hard. She saw Jay first.

"Jay!"

"Hi Mom. Why are you here? I thought you were going to K-Mart."

"Jay, I have to get you all home. I'm getting a migraine. I'll be in the car, please get the others. I'll make it up to you."

"Got it, Mom. We'll hurry."

_____

Jay sighed at the bad luck and ran to find the other three. Zeke was with Jeremy Ting.

"Zeke, Mom is in the car. Migraine coming on. We have to go. I'll get Laura and Sam."

Jeremy said, "Sorry, man. You haven't been here long. I'll be here again tomorrow. Maybe see ya then?"

Zeke and Jay looked at each other and Zeke said, "It's New Year's Eve, so I doubt it. –Gotta go."

Jay put his board in the back of the SUV beside Zeke's and jumped in beside Laura. He explained quickly to her and Sam on the way out, and they seemed to understand.

Zeke was up front and asked Mom, "Hanging in there? Laura drives, if you feel like you can't get us home."

Mom answered, "I think I'll make it, but I have to get to bed ASAP."

Laura and Sam were talking quietly in the back seat when the Enclave abruptly pulled to the side of the road.

Darci said, "I have to close my eyes."

Zeke jumped into action and said, "Mom, you sit here. Laura, can you drive the rest of the way? You're legal and I'm not." He opened his door and got out before opening hers in the back.

Laura got out and said, "I think so. This is bigger than what I'm used to, but I should be okay."

After the seats were switched, Laura pulled back onto the road too slowly and a passing car blared its horn at her.

Zeke offered, "It's cool, don't pay any attention to them. You've got this."

_____

Laura was nervous driving a carload of people in an unfamiliar car. She tried not to let it show, but the honking horn had rattled her. Thank goodness Zeke was calming and encouraging her instead of asking questions like, "Are you sure you know how to drive?"

Darci Munro sat beside her with the seat tilted back and her eyes closed. Once Darci patted her arm and said, "Thank you, Laura."

After what seemed like thirty years to Laura, she pulled in to Munro's drive!

Jay got out and ran to his mom's door to help her out. Laura thought that was sweet of him.

Zeke said, "Thanks, Laura. See you and Sam tomorrow." He started to the back of the vehicle and then stopped. "We can leave our stuff in the back until we go again. Shouldn't be too long."

Mom spent the evening flat on her back sleeping. The next day she came into the kitchen where Zeke and Jay were having breakfast.

"Feeling better today?" Zeke smiled.

"I'm good today. Haven't had one of those in about a year, and almost forgot what it was like. Almost."

CHAPTER TEN

Mom and Dad's dinner reservations were for eight o'clock, and they needed to leave about seven thirty. Dad was okay with Jay and Zeke going next door for a couple hours while they were gone, because Mom had assured him they were up to absolutely nothing, and she thought it was fine.

That's true, Zeke thought. *At least for me. I don't want to have a neighbor for a girlfriend. Besides, Laura is older and Sam's a kid. Nope, they'll make good friends.*

Peppi's pizza was going to be delivered later. As soon as their parents left, Zeke and Jay ran up to the attic with their skateboards to get ready. Zeke had his old red baseball cap on backward and they wore jackets. They worked together to slide boxes out of the way, and Zeke pried the nail out of the wall where Dad had placed it. *No point getting scraped up in the process of testing.*

That nail was the basis of an experiment that had proved that the portal didn't exist for anyone other than the four of them who had recently used it. At least they thought so, because their dad didn't go through it when he had pounded the nail in the wall.

Jay dragged out a ramp that was lying on its side among boxes. Together they fixed it and placed its higher side, which was about two feet high, against the wall. Zeke nodded as he looked at it.

He said, "I know this is an easy trick, but can you believe we're gonna ride our boards through the houses into their attic? It's like we're going through the unknown. Nobody's ever done it before! Not Tony Hawk, not Bob Burnquist, not Rodney Mullen...Nobody!"

Jay said, "Wow, you're right. I hadn't thought about it like that. But nobody will ever know we did this. Nobody will ever see it –or believe it. Too bad, man. We could have been famous. That would be even better than being in the news for saving Sam and Laura."

Zeke laughed, "Yep, but we're dreaming if we think for a second that anyone will know about this. So take it for what it is –a thrill ride we'll always remember."

"I guess you're right, Zeke. Except Laura and Sam will know. And *they'll* believe it because they'll see it for themselves. If I don't marry Laura or Sam, then how will I tell my wife someday that I have a secret with them? I don't think that would go over so well."

Zeke stopped to look at Jay. "Marry Laura? She's a senior in high school and you're in Junior High. And Sam's not your type. You are nuts, man."

Jay objected, "They are *both* my type. End of discussion. You're still going first without your board, to test it, right? Because I'm not doing it if you don't."

Zeke noticed that Jay had put gel in his hair again. *He must want to look good for the girls.* "Yeah, I told Laura I'd call when we were set up, and we'd be doing a test first."

Jay wasn't sure why the addition of a skateboard to the portal made him feel uncomfortable. It was hard enough feeling at ease with the passageway. Part of him liked it, and the other part wished it would go away. He was almost afraid that it would reach out and grab him, pulling him into a place he didn't want to go. *Weird, for sure, but I've heard stories of stranger things, like the Bermuda Triangle. This isn't as scary as that. Plus, Zeke seems fine with it.* Jay's stomach was tied in knots, and he thought it would stay that way until he got it over with. He did not want to act like a chicken.

———————————

Samantha and Laura's parents said it would be okay for them to have the Munro's over while they were at a New Year's Eve party, because the boys had probably saved their daughters' from serious harm, or even death.

    While they were waiting for their parents to leave, Sam put M&M's in a yellow bowl on the table alongside a bag of Sun Chips, her new favorite snack. Pop was in the fridge. She wore another Steelers sweatshirt and jeans.

    Laura was wearing her lavender warm-up set. She pulled her hair back in a pony tail and went to a closet to get out a deck of cards.

As soon as their parents left, Sam and Laura hurried to the attic.

Laura tucked her long auburn hair behind her ear and took out her phone. She called Zeke after she and Sam each pulled a light string in the room. She sat down in the green chair. "Hi, you ready? Test run without a skateboard. Nothing's in the way. See you in a sec." She slipped it back in her hoodie pocket and gave Sam a thumbs-up.

Sam commented, "This is the coolest New Year's Eve *ever*. Too bad we can't tell anyone about it."

The silence as they waited was overwhelming. Suddenly Zeke came through slightly crouched, with his arms out for balance. A red baseball cap with the brim turned backwards was on his head, and he wore an army green shirt.

"Hey, the test run went good! Had to come off the top of the ramp to go through, so I think I have to jump up about two feet and smack the wall to return, so I don't fall over the ramp going back. I'll be right back on my board, and Jay will come after me on his."

Sam said, "That was so cool! You just made history, I think. But maybe there are other portals in the world that nobody can talk about?"

Laura eyed her and replied, "Do you think so? That we don't have the only portal in the world? I never thought about that possibility."

Zeke was impatient to get back. He didn't care about any speculation at the moment. I'm leaving. Bye!" He turned and ran back towards the wall and leaped, tensing up as he hit it and disappeared.

He wasn't there to hear Laura comment, "I'll never get used to seeing people disappear into a wall."

———————————

When Zeke landed at his house his backside hit the incline with a boom. There was no way to totally clear the ramp on the return trip. *Oh well. You only live once... I wish I could be on TV.*

Frowning, Jay asked, "You okay? That return trip was a little messy."

"Yeah, it was worth it. You ready?" Zeke's phone chirped. It was Laura.

"You have to wait a few minutes. Sam said it was too dark in here for me to record it, so she just took off out the door to go get a floor lamp. I'll let you know when we're ready. Oh wow, I hear her coming back up the steps, hold on... She's already back with the lamp. Okay she's gonna plug it in. –We're good!"

Zeke said, "Okay. So you are going to record it?"

"I will unless you don't want me to," Laura answered.

Zeke said, "Record it, please. You'll have to erase it later, but that's okay."

CHAPTER ELEVEN

Jay rolled his skateboard back and forth as Zeke talked. They were ready to ride.

Ending the call, Zeke looked at his brother. "Sam wanted more light and ran to get another lamp. It's set up, and Laura's gonna record it. Ready?"

Swallowing, Jay replied, "Yeah. I'll wait about a minute after you go, so we don't have a pileup."

Zeke slowly skated on the wood floor to the entrance and turned around. There was a nice path between all the attic paraphernalia and boxes. He pulled his hat down and powered off with his right foot as fast as he could and gained momentum.

Zeke felt a rush of exhilaration as his skateboard hit the ramp with his body tucked down as he went air-born toward the portal.

The nose of the skateboard was the first to go into the wall and come through at the Larson's.

He thought he felt his hat fly off, which was odd.

Jay wanted to call Sam and Laura to see if Zeke had made it, but felt that would make him look stupid. It was one thing to jump your way into someone else's attic (how weird was that?), but to fly on a skateboard? Jay worried that might change the end result because of the speed or whatever. He thought that if his brother had somehow skated into the unknown, he must do it too, to be with him. And just maybe to help him if he ran into trouble.

So Jay duplicated everything Zeke just did, and as his board flew down the path in the long room and lifted off the ramp toward the wall, he said a quick prayer.

Standing along the wall in their attic, Laura held the phone steady and had it pointed at the portal wall. Zeke flew into the room with his knees bent and his head low. The board hit the floor and rolled to a stop on the carpet. Zeke popped the board off the floor and caught it. She got the whole thing as Sam clapped and loudly yelled, "Woo-Hoo!"

Zeke looked at them and exclaimed, "Wow! Awesome! Who would believe it?"

Then Zeke said Jay was coming right behind, and scooped up his board and hurried over to get out of the way.

Landing less gracefully when the nose, or front edge of his board came down first, Jay flipped and rolled off the front. "Whoa…!" When the motion stopped, he was about four feet from his board and lying on his side.

Zeke went over and gave him a hand up. "You did it, Bro. You glad they have carpet?"

Jay grabbed Zeke's hand and jumped to his feet. "It needs more padding. That was a gnarly ride! I can't believe I did this."

All four high-fived and laughed. Zeke said, "I want to do it one more time, maybe with more speed. Jay?"

"Nope. Once is enough. Boarding portals is not for me. Hey, where's your hat?" He pointed to Zeke's head.

Zeke touched his hair and blinked, "You're right. I thought I felt it fly off. I'll get it next time around." He looked to the other three and smiled. "Back in a few. Keep the area clear!" He put his board under his arm and went up to the wall and jumped high up into it as he slapped it.

Sam looked at Jay and Laura and said, "Back to safety," as she headed out of the way. She continued, "You know, I'd like to go through the portal one more time before it closes too, just not on a skateboard."

With a shrug, Laura responded, "Why not? Go for it. Just don't ask me, because I've had my one and only trip, and I'm done." Laura was so done with portals.

Then they were quiet, knowing it was about time for Zeke. They sat together on the floor and watched.

When Zeke came through that time he was sitting even lower, and was definitely going faster. The board hit the carpet hard. Zeke popped it, flipped and caught it.

Cheers erupted.

"Thanks." He placed the skateboard near Jay's. "You know, my baseball hat wasn't over there." He turned his head around looking for it in the Larson's attic.

Sam said, "I watched you skate through the first time, and you did *not* have a hat. But you did during the jump-through test at the beginning." She frowned at him.

Speaking up, Jay declared, "I *know* he had it on, because he pulled it down on his head before taking off." He looked at his brother quizzically, "You checked everywhere in our attic?"

Zeke said, "It's not there."

Sam said, "I feel like looking outside between our two houses."

Jay responded, "That's exactly how I felt once, and I did look there when the red duffel bag went through. There was nothing in the yard of course, because it landed here in your attic." Jay raised his arms and shrugged.

Zeke bit his lower lip and said, "That is my favorite hat, but it's not that important. Pizza's coming at 8:45, which is pretty soon.

"Jay, let's get our boards home and get these coats off. Then we'll go to their front door like normal people with the pizza."

"I'm following you through," Sam said. "I just want to do it one more time before it closes."

Zeke said, "Fine, but I'll go first and move the ramp so you won't have to jump."

Laura watched them go one at a time. Sam went after a few minutes, to give them time to clear the ramps out of the way. She shivered and waited for her sister's return.

Samantha was excited to go through the portal again, even if it wasn't as a skateboard rider. Zeke and Jay had moved things as promised, and then made very quick work of putting their attic back the way it was. She walked around looking, but she didn't see a hat anywhere.

Cleaning up took about five minutes, and the boys were done. Samantha waved goodbye and hit their attic wall for the last time. She hoped.

CHAPTER TWELVE

On their way back down to the main floor Jay said, "I was looking at her face. That must've really hurt."

"I think so, too. She's tough."

It was about nine o'clock when they rang the Larson's doorbell. So much had gone on in the last hour that Zeke felt it was surreal.

"Come in!" Sam grinned and took the two pizzas from Zeke. "Leave your shoes here, and you can toss your coats wherever you want. Laura's in the kitchen." She walked to the kitchen and put the pizzas on the counter top.

Laura said to her sister, "We have maybe an hour before they have to leave. Better eat and look at the recording so I can erase it. There isn't enough time to play cards.

Zeke walked through the living room behind Sam, looking around as he went. The rooms were set up the same as his house, but with different colors and furniture.

Sam was taking ice out of the freezer for their drinks, and must have noticed him looking around. She said, "I've been in your attic and down the stairs to your living room, but not in your kitchen. What color is it?"

"Huh?"

Sam said, "How is your kitchen different, although it's the same?

Jay said almost under his breath, "Well, for one thing, we had four kids killed in our kitchen."

Laura dropped a glass and it fell on the floor. "Oh!"

Zeke picked it up. It hadn't even cracked. He said, "Jay, come on."

Sam interjected, "It's okay. I wondered if you thought about that very often. I was only talking about colors and stuff. Guess it doesn't matter, really."

Zeke didn't want things to get depressing. There was too much of that in his life. He joked, "Our kitchen?" He went to the refrigerator and opened it. "Let's see, you have blueberry yogurt. We hate yogurt. And you have Swiss cheese. We have American."

Laura laughed, "I don't think that's what Sam is talking about, but thanks for lightening things up. Sam, we need the pizza cutter. The cheese has melted over where they cut it."

"Got it."

Zeke did wonder how things could look so different in identical houses. It occurred to him that the outside sameness of the houses meant nothing, just like with people – you couldn't just look at someone and know what was inside them.

Handing him a glass, Laura asked, "You don't like the decorating?"

"No, I do, but it hit me that you don't know what's on the other side of someone's front door until you walk in."

Laura didn't comment and busied herself with napkins and plates.

She poured pop into his glass, and Zeke watched it fizz.

There was an awkward silence.

Zeke turned and opened a pizza box and pulled out a slice.

Jay blurted, "We're going to move."

At the same time, Sam and Laura both asked, "What?"

Jay continued, "Dad says not to tell Mom about what happened in our house in 1959 or she'll freak. He said he's going to look for another house first, and he already saw one he might be interested in."

"Please keep that to yourselves." Zeke chomped on his pizza.

Laura said, "I'm really sorry to hear that. It's been nice having you guys next door.

If you hadn't been there, we might be dead now."

Sam seemed to take it better and said, "I don't blame him. Who knows, maybe we'll move too, because my mother said she doesn't know if she can get over McIntyre being in here and hurting us. Not to mention a gun and money hiding here all those years. I think she's afraid there's more drama to come. Dunno." She took a bite of pizza as she eased herself into a chair at the small table. Laura looked at Jay and asked, "Did he say where this house was?"

"Yeah. He said the address was 322 Romman. I remembered that because I used to have a math class back in Phoenix in room 322. Romman Court or Avenue –not sure which. Do you know where that is?"

Laura shook her head and said, "Maybe. I think it's clear on the other side of town." She wiped her hands and popped two green M&M's in her mouth.

Zeke looked around for a clock and asked, "How are we looking time-wise? 'Cause I want to see the video of the portal ride if you don't mind."

Laura's ponytail flipped as she jumped out of her chair and headed to get her phone from the counter. She was back in a flash and knelt down between Jay and Zeke's chairs and held the screen in front of them on the table. Sam came around and leaned over Laura's shoulder to see.

Laura said, "No greasy fingers on this, please."

The screen showed Zeke rolling across the floor on his board and then popping it up and catching it. There was no entrance from the wall. That was immediately followed by Jay's board accident, but it didn't show him coming out of the wall, either.

Sam chuckled, "Nice landing, Jay. That'll probably be me when I start taking lessons."

Jay asked, "Man, I hope not. But did you notice? It didn't show either of us coming out of the portal wall."

They were all silent for a few seconds before Zeke asked, "I noticed. Did you record it the second time I went through?"

"No, only the first time."

Sam shook her head and commented, "Leaving the portal can't be seen at all."

Zeke scratched his chin. "I guess not. That's incredible." He was in awe and disappointed at the same time.

Laura said, "I'm still going to erase it. How would we explain you guys on skateboards in the attic?"

Sam nodded in agreement. "It's probably going to close forever on the 5th, when Jay has his birthday. I guess I'm glad."

"I *know* I'm glad." Laura closed her eyes and sighed like the portal was already going away.

Jay added, "Me, too."

They looked at Zeke. A few seconds later he said, "Not sure how I feel about it now." He shrugged and inserted three carefully stacked Sun Chips into his mouth.

Sam asked, "Do you think everything's all wrapped up now?"

Zeke's bangs slid onto his forehead, which reminded him again about his missing ball cap. *Where did it go?* He shuddered slightly. "I think it will be wrapped up when I find the hat. That bothers me. If you find an old red hat, it has Z-O-O-M written inside the band."

"Zoom? What's that mean?" Sam asked.

Jay answered, "That was his baseball name. The Z is for Zeke, and M is for Munro. He could zoom around the bases faster than anyone."

Zeke's phone vibrated and he looked at it. Mom and Dad were home. "Thanks for letting us come. The parents are home." He took his empty glass to the sink.

Laura nodded and smiled, "Yeah, it was fun."

Sam added, "You know, *whatever* happens on the 5th, you guys are still our friends. Thank you."

Zeke patted her head like a dog and said, "You're welcome." Sam looked a little pathetic with her cut and bruised cheek. She was growing on him. He remembered how much he disliked her and how angry he'd been when she "dropped" into his attic on his birthday.

That day began the portal adventure and Jay's birthday would possibly end it. He wildly hoped that it might not. But don't all good things eventually come to an end? He had assumed that the portal was a good thing. *It is, isn't it?*

CHAPTER THIRTEEN

It was New Year's Day, and Darcie Munro said she'd take the kids back to Breeze for a redo.

Samantha was upset. Although she and Laura were allowed to go again, her mother said she could not sign up and take a skating lesson. "But Mom, why can't I do a lesson today?"

"Because I haven't seen Breeze. I'd have to personally sign waiver papers. I'd have to pay, too, and we still have stuff to catch up on after Christmas. It's just not happening right now for all those reasons. Now I have to get to work."

Samantha slumped over the arm of the sofa and dropped her back onto the seat cushions. "Great."

Mom said, "I have to go now. You can't always get what you want when you want it."

It wasn't often that Samantha felt sorry for herself, but this was one of those days.

Laura came into the living room. "What's wrong with you?"

"I'm not allowed to do skatepark lessons yet. I was hoping to start today."

Laura stared. "Well maybe you're too old to learn anyway. I know I am. Better be ready to go. They're leaving soon."

Samantha rolled sideways off the sofa and flopped onto the floor. She pictured how she looked doing it and started laughing. "Okay. I'm ready."

Laura said, "What? Aren't you going to put on something nice?"

"What's wrong with my Steelers sweatshirt?"

"I should have known better than to ask. Let's go."

On the way there, Darcie said, "I'm glad this worked out for everybody today. I felt so bad making you leave last time."

Samantha said, "It's okay, really. I've never had a migraine and don't want one."

"Thanks for understanding. I'm gonna try to go to K-Mart again and some other places. Maybe five hours at the most."

Zeke said, "That works. Thanks. Jay, this time get a punch-card so you can eventually get a free trip. I got a card last time so I'm one punch ahead."

Jay said, "I'll give you another one, haha!"

Laura responded, "I doubt I'll be here much after today. I don't plan on getting on a skateboard. No offense. Besides, I have to conserve money."

Darcie asked her, "What do you plan to do after graduation?"

"I'd like to have my own boutique. Sell pretty collectibles and gently used lamps, end tables and things like that. I already have a collection of mixed colored glassware and small things to sell, stashed at my grandma's. It fills a whole bedroom at her place, and part of her basement."

Samantha added, "She's got cool stuff stacked to the ceiling in there. Enter at your own risk!"

Darcie commented, "You sound like you know what you want, Laura. I wish you great success. I'll shop at your store."

Zeke turned partly around to ask, "Not going to college?"

"I'll take business and marketing night classes, but that will be part time. I've researched this for a couple years, and it's what I want to do."

Jay said, "Cool. Can I work for you? I count change and inventory at my dad's store."

Zeke joked, "You *eat* the inventory at Dad's store."

"Hey, knock it off."

Darcie interjected, "Yes, knock it off, Zeke."

•   "Okay, I'm sorry. Mom, can you buy a basketball at K-Mart while you're there? I have to give one to David Mellon before I forget and he tries to tackle me again. I'll pay you back."

Jay blurted, "And by the way, he tried to give *my* basketball to him!"

Darcie exclaimed, "What?"

"Yeah, Zeke tried to give my ball to the guy. Can you believe it?" Jay leaned forward and smacked the back of Zeke's seat.

Samantha flinched when Zeke literally shouted, "I *said* I was sorry!"

Darcie slowed the car and pulled over. She said, "Why don't you guys jump out and talk it over while we wait?"

Samantha held her breath and glanced over at Laura. Jay was sitting beside her by the window. He opened his door and got out on the side of the road, and so did Zeke. There was no way she was watching them out there.

Darci said, "Sorry, we do this when things get loud. It'll only take a minute. They argue and fight a lot."

———————————

Zeke felt like such a jerk. He wanted to get the argument over with quickly.

Jay glared at him. "Look what you started. You didn't have to say how much I eat!

And you didn't have to try to give my basketball away."

Zeke argued, "And you didn't have to bring the basketball thing up in front of anybody and embarrass *me*."

"You embarrassed yourself when you yelled."

"Okay, Jay. You're right. I was wrong to make fun of your eating in front of them. And like I told you the other day, I'm sorry about the basketball. Is that enough to make you happy?"

Jay replied, "You don't have to be sarcastic."

"Alright. I'm sorry about the basketball. We good now? Let's get to Breeze before we waste any more time."

Jay sighed, "Ok, we're good. Too bad you don't get to sit next to Laura...haha."

"Why you– she's just a friend, and be quiet so they don't hear."

Jay laughed and ran to the car and jumped in.

Zeke noted how the mood in the car changed for the better the rest of the way. He and Jay always argued and fought about things. It had been better between them lately because of the shared portal secret.

When they got to Breeze Mom didn't come in because waivers were already on file for them. Her only comment was, "Stay in twos and do not leave here for any reason until all four of you go to lunch together. I'll be back around 3:00."

CHAPTER FOURTEEN

They walked through the door at Breeze to hear the Bee Gee's hit song, "Stayin' Alive." Jay immediately started to lip-sync and dance.

Sam laughed, "Hey, watch out. I don't want to get smacked with your skateboard. I'm still healing up."

"Oh," he said, "I wouldn't want that to happen."

Zeke led toward the counter and paid for himself and got his card punched. Jay did the same after he asked for a card.

Zeke asked, "Will you hang onto our water for us?" He slipped two bottles to Laura and Jay dug a bottle out of his coat and gave it to Samantha.

Samantha could feel the heartbeat of the place again and smiled to herself. "Here, I'm hanging my coat up. Let me take yours, too."

The boys thanked her and hurried off to warm up.

Samantha watched the boards and bikes doing flips and tricks. It was constant motion, and as the music played, riders stayed out of each other's way as much as possible. She loved to hear the clack of a board going down and the hum of wheels moving.

Not so fun to see was when somebody wiped out in an epic stunt fail that had to hurt. Then there were a few cautious people who weren't as brave to try things. She knew that's where she'd be if she ever made it from the beginner room to this room. In her head, she was doing it all, though.

Samantha stayed with Laura part of the time, but not so much when Laura was talking with other people. Then she felt like the little sister hanging around, although Laura didn't treat her like that around people. Laura told her why last week.

A friend of Laura's lost her little sister in an accident with a horse, and she'd told Laura to cherish her sister, because now she wished that she had, but it was too late.

Zeke, Jay, Laura and Samantha left Breeze temporarily for lunch at one o'clock. They got their Arby's food and sat down together.

Zeke said, "Mom said she'd be back to get us at 3:00. We may be able to get rides in the future with Jeremy, 'cause he's got a car."

Jay said, "Seriously? That's great."

Laura said, "It's a long day when you're just standing around like me, not that I've minded being here. I made a couple new friends." She flipped her long auburn hair behind her shoulders and bit into a slider.

Samantha said, "I noticed. Anyone from school?'

Laura said, "Jeremy Ting is the only one I knew, but there's another guy I recognized. Jay, what do you have in your hair?"

Jay replied, "It's still there?" He bent over away from the table and brushed his hands through his short, brown spiked hair. A little piece of white crumbly stuff fell to the floor. "Some white stuff fell on my head when I was in the bathroom. I think the ceiling tile is crumbling. I tried to shake it out of my hair. Kinda ruins my look, ya know?" He smiled impishly.

Samantha thought Jay was funny, and didn't mind his goofy ways. She said, "Lucky the whole tile didn't fall on your head, Jay. The women's bathroom ceiling looked fine. A little dreary, but fine. I read a true story once about a janitor who went in the men's room and stood on the counter to reach the ceiling. He lifted an acoustic tile up and hoisted himself up in there and then put the tile back. Then he crawled across the ceiling and spied down into the women's bathroom. He got some serious jail time for that and was labeled a predator. Eww!"

Laura added, "Ew is right. I remember hearing about it. Disgusting. Glad they caught him."

Jay added, "That's a weirdo."

Samantha noticed that Zeke seemed lost in thought. "What are you thinking, Zeke?"

Zeke blinked. "Three slightly-off things. Maybe nothing, but that Mason Smythe boy is missing, so maybe these three things are connected."

Samantha sat forward. "What? Is the missing helmet one of them?" She explained to Jay and Laura how it had vanished the day before yesterday when they were at Breeze.

Zeke said, "Yes, the missing helmet. And before that, Jeremy had a sticker stuck to the bottom of his shoe. He picked it up went he went for a bathroom break."

Laura said, "A sticker?"

Zeke went on, "Yeah, a sticker. It was a torn label for a camping toilet."

Laura laughed, "What? They have real toilets in the women's room. Don't they have them in the men's?"

Zeke laughed, "Yes, of course they do. That's why it's strange. Why would a product sticker like that be here?"

Samantha asked, "So what's the third strange thing?"

Zeke looked at Jay and said, "The acoustic ceiling tile piece in his hair. I was in the bathroom, and nothing fell on my head. And Jeremy was there and only came out with a sticker on his shoe. Nothing in his braids."

Samantha asked, "So do you think that the helmet was hidden up in the ceiling, or that there is someone hiding in the ceiling, like the guy I talked about?" She shivered and gulped.

Zeke responded, "I don't know. There's a kid missing. You found a helmet with a name that matches his, which could be nothing really, but then the helmet disappears. Then there's the camping toilet. And ceiling tile crumbs in his hair." He pointed to Jay.

Jay said, "So what if that sticker was on Jeremy's shoe?"

Samantha said, "I think Zeke may be right about that being more than strange, because why would a sticker for a camping toilet show up inside this place?"

Laura said, "I'm with Jay. So what?"

Zeke said, "I'm not trying to be Sherlock Holmes, and I'll probably be embarrassed about this later, BUT if someone was holding a hostage, they might need a toilet for the hostage."

Samantha said, "Oh, my, you're right! Let's eat fast and get back there. Are you going to tell anybody about this?"

Zeke said, "Only Jeremy. We can all do some snooping around, but let's do it in two's because there's less chance of trouble that way."

Laura agreed, "Have each other's backs, I get that, but why don't we call the police?"

Zeke said, "I don't think we have enough evidence, if we have any at all. The helmet is gone, remember? And it could have belonged to any kid named Mason."

Samantha smiled and said sarcastically, "Yeah, like there are lots of Masons who come to this skatepark."

Zeke rolled his eyes. "Let Jay and I check out the ceiling first. If we find anything suspicious, we'll call the police."

They dove into what food was left and hurried back to Breeze.

CHAPTER FIFTEEN

Back at Breeze, Zeke filled Jeremy in on what they talked about at lunch. Then he and Jay went to the men's room to check out the ceiling.

Zeke said, "I'll lock the restroom door, but if someone is impatient, tell them I'm puking or something. I'll stand on the sink, lift the ceiling tile, and look around. Shouldn't take long."

Jay nodded, "Got it, Bro."

Zeke saw a tiny piece of tile on the sink counter. He jumped up on the sink and lifted the ceiling tile with his fingertips. The top part of his face went up into the ceiling –just enough for his eyes to be able to see two things that surprised him. The area was dimly lit, and there was a narrow lightweight ladder lying down across the ceiling supports. *Someone has been going in and out of here!* He couldn't see anything else except a metal support that ran alongside a ventilation duct. *Just wide enough to crawl along without falling through the ceiling.* Zeke was going to pull the ladder down and use it to get up into that area when he heard Jay talking to someone outside the door.

"Someone's in there. Sounds like he's puking his guts out!"

A male voice said, "I don't care what he's doing. I work here and I'm going in."

Zeke put the tile in place and jumped down *just* as the lock popped and the door opened. Zeke bent to turn on the spigot. He nonchalantly splashed running water on his face, and then turned to see who the pushy visitor was.

The guy was an employee. Zeke saw him earlier emptying a trash can. He was about twenty, and he had curly black hair and an eyebrow piercing.

He didn't say anything to Zeke, but Zeke noticed his eyes darted around the bathroom, and briefly up to the ceiling.

The man said, "Heard you were sick. You okay, man?"

Zeke answered, "The water in my face helps. I think I can ride some more now. Thanks." Zeke walked past him and into the hall, where Jay's eyes were bugged out like a frog's.

Zeke grabbed his elbow and put a finger to his lips. "Shhh. Follow me."

When they reached the first big skating area, Zeke glanced around before saying to Jay, "Yeah, someone's been going in and out through the ceiling. It's probably the guy who wanted in the bathroom. Thanks for stalling him."

Jay said, "Yeah, he was pushy and acted suspicious. What do we do now?"

Zeke answered, "I want to skate and think on it. I'll come up with something."

Jay said, "Okay. Laura and Sam are walking around, and I hope they see or hear something. I think I'd like to be a private investigator someday, you know?"

Zeke looked at his brother with the brown spikes and his chubby cheeks, and said, "Fine, but I'm not working for you. After that McIntyre thing, I'm done with solving things, unless of course we find out something about Mason Smythe and can help him. I wonder if he's somewhere in this building? It's a big place. Keep your voice down if you talk to the Larson's." He put down his board and pushed off.

———————————

Meanwhile, Sam and Laura looked through all the used equipment for anything else that might have the name Mason on it, or to see if the blue helmet had reappeared. They came up with zilch.

Samantha said, "Nothing here. Let's casually walk around and peek in any doors we find."

"Okay, but I don't want people looking at us wondering what we're doing."

Breeze Skatepark took up a lot of space, with the store, halls, restrooms, and three different skating areas.

Laura said, "Let's start in the little kids' side. I haven't seen it yet, anyway."

On the way down the hallway to it, Samantha stopped by a brown metal door. "I wonder where this leads? I think I'll take a look."

Laura stepped in front of her and said, "No. You are still healing up. I'll look in there. You be the watcher." Laura couldn't get past Sam's face being so banged up, and even though her sister was tough, she didn't look tough at the moment.

Sam sighed, "Okay."

Laura looked right and left, saw nobody coming and opened the door. She flipped on the light and looked around. She whispered, "A mop, bucket, cleaning rags and supplies. It's just a closet with another door that must be to another closet or something. Keep watch, while I look into it." Samantha nodded at her and closed the outer door.

Laura opened the second door.

A strong arm reached out and grabbed her and slapped a gloved hand over her mouth! She tried to scream, but the hand held firm. She could smell the glove's leather. When she tried to pull away, her long red hair was yanked hard and her head went back. Her captor's face was covered by a ski mask.

Whoever held her closed the door and locked it, and roughly turned her in the opposite direction. He had the back of her hair in his grasp, and his other hand clamped tightly on her face as he pushed her forward in semi-darkness. Laura was petrified.

All she could think of was that Gerald McIntyre had escaped from jail and tracked her down. As her attacker pushed her forward and down each step, tears streamed from her eyes and she tried to scream against the leather glove over her mouth.

They half-stumbled down steps as he held her firmly from behind and propelled her along. Her only hope was that Sam had gone for help!

CHAPTER SIXTEEN

Zeke was doing some easy riding, trying to decide what to do about what he knew so far. Did they know enough to call the police? It didn't seem like it. He was coming out of the half pipe when Jay flew by on his board and hissed, "Got trouble. Sam needs us now. Laura's disappeared!"

Zeke popped his board and jumped off. He hurried behind Jay to where Sam stood looking frantic. "Tell us what happened!"

Sam gulped and trembled, "I was standing outside of a closet that Laura went into. It had an interior door that she was going to check out. After a few minutes, I went into the closet and she was gone. I tried that inner door, but it was locked from the other side. She's just vanished! *We need to call the police!*"

Zeke was already pulling his phone out of his jeans. "I agree. Jay, here, take my phone and call the police, then Mom. Wait for the police by the entrance. Sam, show me where Laura disappeared, and then run back and wait with Jay for the cops and Mom. And call your parents!"

Sam nodded at him and took off toward the little kids' end of Breeze.

When they got there, she opened the door and showed him the locked inner door. Zeke said, "I can't break it down. I have another idea. Jay will know it has to do with the men's restroom. You get back to him and wait for the police."

Zeke watched Sam go in the direction of the entrance, and he hurried toward the hall where the men's room was. Once inside the bathroom, he jumped up on the sink and lifted the acoustic tile. He pulled the ladder down and climbed up so he could get into the ceiling, being careful to keep his body weight on the

127

metal support by the ductwork as he crawled along. He lifted the ladder going up from the bathroom into the ceiling. He was certain that Jay would figure it out and lead the police there. *Gotta find Laura. I hope this leads to her!*

Zeke crawled as fast as he dared for about sixty feet. Along the way, he passed bottles of water, boxes of crackers, a pillow, and a black trash bag with something in it. He came to an abrupt drop off. There was an industrial ladder bolted to the wall. Before he climbed down it, he scanned a huge grey room. Small windows about thirty feet up let in light. He didn't see anyone. There were stacks of wooden pallets, an old fork lift, some tires, and what looked like it might be a warehouse office. It was completely boxed in like an office would be. Zeke climbed down the ladder to the ground and kept low, making his way toward the "office."

Still not seeing anyone, Zeke tried the door. It was locked. He thought he heard stirring on the other side. He stepped back and placed an ear on the wall. Then he heard something else. *Someone is coming. . .*

He dove behind the pallets just in time. He couldn't see who it was, but he heard footsteps coming in his direction. His head tucked, crouching low, he thought he heard struggling near the door. Scuffling and the sound of keys . . . Zeke peaked around the stacked pallets and saw Laura being shoved into the room! She shouted, "You won't get away with this!" The door slammed shut, muffling her cries, and the masked man was putting a key into the lock when Zeke lunged from behind and slammed his masked face hard into the door.

Bam! The man crumpled to the ground.

Zeke grabbed the keys from the gloved hand and unlocked the door.

A leather-fringed boot flew out and knocked Zeke over backward!

Zeke yelled, "Laura, stop! It's me!"

"Ah! Oh –I'm sorry! Zeke! I'm sorry. *Thank you*. Am I glad to see *you*!"

Zeke picked himself up off the dusty floor, and a teary Laura hugged him. She said, "There's a boy in there. I think we found Mason Smythe!"

She turned toward the office as a boy came out and looked at the man lying on the ground. He trembled as he tip-toed past and stood near Zeke and Laura.

"Th-th-thank you."

Zeke asked, "Are you Mason?"

"Y-yes. That guy was keeping me here. I never saw his face, and he never talked to me."

The boy disappeared into the office and came back holding a coffee mug. He said, "We can hit him with this if he wakes up."

"What if he does wake up? What can we do besides hit him with a coffee cup?" Laura had her arms folded across her middle and backed away from the man on the floor.

Zeke couldn't help but smile. "Sam called the police, and they will come. In the meantime, I'll knock him out if I have to. He's not gonna just jump up without giving us warning."

Laura asked the boy, "Are you okay?"

"Yeah, I guess so. I'm really glad to get out of there. Thank you."

Suddenly double doors in an outside wall burst open and four policemen with guns drawn and pointed at them fanned out.

Zeke slowly put his hands up, and so did Mason and Laura.

Zeke said, "This is Mason Smythe. He was being kept in that room by the guy on the floor."

One cop bent to cuff the man's wrists pat him down for weapons. The mask was yanked off.

Mason took a step back. "It's Victor!"

Zeke wasn't shocked to see it was the employee who had unlocked the restroom door when he was in there snooping. His nose was all bloody from Zeke's smash-up on the door, but he was beginning to move.

———————————————

Mr. and Mrs. Smythe got there with the FBI forty minutes later. Zeke's mom was back at Breeze and pale as a ghost. Georgia Larson was on her way to get Sam and Laura. Laura was fine. Zeke thought it wasn't necessary for Mrs. Larson to come, because the girls could ride home with them. After all, they were neighbors. But try telling that to a worried mother.

Zeke could hardly believe everything that had happened. If he'd known about all the adventures awaiting him in Indiana before he moved from Phoenix, he might not have been so upset about the move.

I stopped Gerald McIntyre, a murderer, we are getting actual reward money, and now I caught a kidnapper and rescued Mason Smythe! Holy smokes!

CHAPTER SEVENTEEN

Laura said, "Look, we're on the front page of the news again! "**Mason Smythe Found, Kidnapper Captured.**"

Samantha looked over her shoulder and shook her head. "I still can't believe it. Hey, it says you got kidnapped, too. And Zeke rescued you and Mason. Don't you feel like life is *crazy*?"

Laura agreed, "No joke. When will it be NORMAL again?"

Samantha responded, "I think it will be when the portal closes, and that should be at midnight as time changes to January 5th when Jay turns fourteen. Then the numbers that opened the portal will change."

Laura added, "I hope so! I'm gonna pretend it's already closed. I can't stand all of this."

Samantha nodded, "I hear you. It's been too much lately, and yesterday you had a bad shake-up. Laura, I'm so glad you weren't hurt. He could have thrown you down those stairs and dragged you to that room."

Laura tossed the newspaper and said, "Me too. I still feel shaky inside. Kinda afraid. And Mom and Dad just went backward in time five years in how they're treating me today. It's like they're afraid something else will happen. First, you get injured the day after Christmas by *Gerald*, and then I go and get temporarily kidnapped by Victor. Ugh! Will they ever let us out of their sight again?"

———————

Jay watched Zeke dig in a kitchen cupboard. He asked, "What're you looking for?"

Zeke replied, "I'm gonna make a cake for David Mellon."

"You're making a *cake*? For a guy who jumps you?" Jay doubled over, howling with laughter.

Jay didn't see the cake mix coming before it hit him in the behind and Zeke was all over him. Jay yelled, "Stop! What did I doooo?"

Dad came running into the kitchen and saved him. "What's all this about?"

Zeke was sprawled on the floor. Jay jumped up and hid behind Dad. Jay said, "I think Zeke has been through a lot lately and might need counseling."

Zeke narrowed his eyes and said, "Why you . . ."

"Stop," Dad ordered. "Tell me what's going on."

Zeke brushed his bangs back and got to his feet. "I snapped. I'm sorry. You okay, Jay?"

Jay answered, "You didn't hurt me. Apology accepted."

Dad asked, "Why is that cake mix on the floor? You two fighting over it?"

Zeke started to laugh, which surprised Jay. Maybe his brother *was* cracking up?

Zeke stopped and said, "Dad, everything's okay. I was going to make a cake for the neighbor who's jumped me twice – David Mellon– to make peace with him once and for all. I gave him candy a few days ago, but he still seemed like he didn't trust me. And then Jay comes in and starts laughing at me. But I guess it could be funny. Sorry."

Dad said, "I think the cake is a great idea. When I think about all that's happened to you lately . . . stopping Gerald McIntyre, David Mellon going after you, and yesterday catching the kidnapper –I think *I* need counseling! It makes my head spin."

Jay knew it was true, and Dad didn't even know about the portal. "Zeke, I'm sorry I laughed about it. I'll go with you when you take the new basketball and cake to him."

Dad added, "And it's not over, because Zeke will have to testify against that Victor guy if he doesn't plead guilty. So will Laura. It's a good thing McIntyre confessed, or you'd have both been in court for that. I think the old guy wanted to go back to prison after he was caught."

Zeke asked, "Dad, will you bring home a newspaper when you get back from the store? I'm saving certain news articles these days."

Dad laughed, "Sure, and I can't *imagine* which ones you're saving."

CHAPTER EIGHTEEN

Early in the morning on January fifth, Samantha got out of bed and grabbed her purple terry robe and tied the belt. It was still dark out as she crept up to the attic. She'd wanted to test the portal the night before, but couldn't risk it because she knew Zeke's parents were home and might be up until after midnight. No, she decided the best time would be when everyone in both houses was still sound asleep.

Her parents had firmly refused to let her take skateboard lessons at Breeze. After what had happened to Laura and Mason, she couldn't blame them.

She walked into the attic, pulled the two light strings. She saw the floor lamp that she'd taken upstairs the night before, and made a mental note to take it back down after checking the portal.

Standing in front of the portal area, Samantha stared at "the wall." It was just a wall like any other. She drew in her breath and raised her right hand and hit it. The hard surface stung her palm. Her curls bounced as she hit it several more times in different places to be sure. *It's closed!*

Samantha wasn't sure how she really felt deep inside, but she thought she was happy about it. She looked down at the floor as she turned to go, and noticed her little red plastic dog was lying by the wall under the window where the detective left him, before the money stolen by McIntyre was found inside the wall. *Was that really less than a week ago?*

She scooped him up and whispered, "Let's go tell Laura." Slipping him into the pocket of her robe, she unplugged the floor lamp and wrapped the cord so it wouldn't drag as she took it downstairs.

Zeke was the only one awake at his house. He tried his side of the portal, and found that it was closed. He went back to his room, sat at his desk and clicked on a black metal desk lamp. Shaking his head to clear it, his hair fell down over his face. He he sat there thinking.

His phone was on the charger near him and he heard a notification that he'd just received a text. Unplugging the phone, Zeke picked it up. It was from Sam. *She's up early, too.*

The message said, "Portal is closed. I checked."

He texted. "Right. I checked it too. Are we happy about that?"

A couple minutes went by and then Sam texted him again, "Don't know...Did you ever find your hat?"

Zeke looked at the question on his screen and paused momentarily. His stomach did a little flip before he responded, "No."

Someone shook her shoulder. Laura rolled over in bed and opened her eyes.

It was Sam. She whispered, "Guess what, the portal is closed! Zeke checked his side, too – do you believe it?"

Laura's heart beat faster as she focused on what she was hearing. She blinked a few times and fingered stray hair off her face. "Thank you, God! I have my life back! She threw back her quilt and sat up. "There's school tomorrow and I can have a regular life again! Hooray!"

Jay woke up knowing it was his fourteenth birthday. He lay there thinking about the theory that the portal would be closed today because certain numbers would no longer line up. *That's a good birthday present!*

Zeke walked into his room. "The portal is closed. I tried it from here, and Sam tried it from their side."

Jay sat up in bed. "Great!"

"There's just one thing, Jay."

Jay saw that Zeke didn't look too happy about the portal news. "What? What's wrong, Zeke?"

"My red baseball hat is nowhere. It's gone."

Jay joked, "You'll get another hat. It's no big deal. Maybe the portal swallowed it."

Zeke looked at him. "The portal never "swallowed" anything before. I think it means something."

Jay fell back on his pillow, pulled the covers over his head and kicked and shouted, "Why can't we have *normal* birthdays in Indiana?!"

Coming next:

The Journey

www.revelstreet.com

nealierose.com

.

54279176R00083

Made in the USA
Columbia, SC
30 March 2019